Come Close

A NOVELLA BY FELICIA PRIDE

ISBN (paperback): 979-8-9991402-1-0
ISBN (eBook): 979-8-9991402-0-3

Published by HONEY CHILE Entertainment
www.honey-chile.com

Printed in the United States of America
First Edition

To my first love, you know who you are.

TABLE OF CONTENTS

CHAPTER 1:
TAKEOFF

AMAYA

"Do you want to hold my hand?" Chloe jokingly asks me as she blows up her *Law & Order*-branded neck pillow that we got years ago as a wrap gift. She can be nostalgic like that. Me? I like to move the F on. Next stop. Rearview loading. That was so yesterday.

We're on our first class flight from Los Angeles to Baltimore and I've just finished wiping down every nasty crevice of my seat, its back pocket, the tray table, my seat belt and am now saying a silent prayer with my eyes closed. But I open one of them to side-eye my homegirl and business partner. She thinks my disdain for flying is ridiculous. Whereas I think the blood red Stacy Adams fedora that she's wearing is *actually* ridiculous, especially paired with a vintage Jordache jumpsuit. But Chloe's confidence stays at a thousand. Helps that she's classically gorgeous in a Diahann Carroll way, even resembling her. A glamorous cocoa face with soft notes. And a wig to match whatever mood she's in. She's rocking a bob under the hat, which means she's feeling froggy.

"You do realize that in the last two weeks, there have been four plane crashes in the U.S.?" I quip with the sharp judgement of a church mother.

"Oh." She waves me off with her jeweled-nailed hand. "That's because the evil pumpkin-faced dictator fired a bunch of people at the FAA."

"We should have taken the train." It's a ridiculous suggestion, but I don't flinch.

"Across the country?"

"I hear the views are amazing."

"We don't have time for the train. You know why?" Chloe smiles like a sneaky teenager. And I can't help but do the same.

"Because we're shooting my first feature film," I answer proudly. After years toiling in Hollywood as a TV writer and director, selling shows and films that were never made because "they weren't universal enough," stomaching Ls from people who reside in a Tesla bubble, telling a bunch of stories about white people falling in love over a surgery table or while patrolling the mean streets, I'm finally on the precipice of my personal holy grail. At 42 years old.

Directing a *great* first feature film can put you on a life-changing path toward mo' money, mo' opportunity, mo' agency, and most importantly, mo' freedom. Think Dee Rees and *Pariah*. Ryan Coogler and *Fruitvale Station*. Spike Lee and *She's Gotta Have It*. Kasi Lemmons and *Eve's*

Bayou. I could keep going. And it would be a dream to add Amaya Ellis and *Slow Down, More Time* to the list.

Bottom line: I want to have the power and leverage to dictate my future, where Chloe and I build our production company Double Magic (because it's two Black girls) into an indie powerhouse where we attract our own financing to make film and television projects by, for, or about Black women. Light work.

"Exactly, bitch! Because we're shooting your first feature film." Thank God for Chloe's perpetual optimism. She and I met as production assistants (P.A.s) on one of the million *CSI* spinoffs. I was wet behind the Hollywood ears and Chloe taught me how to properly use a walkie talkie. She had a few years on me, but we bonded because we were more than dreamers. We were obsessed with catching said dreams. Chips on our shoulders? Perhaps. Deep, unhealthy desire to prove folk wrong? Definitely. There aren't many who understand that to us, especially as single badasses with no kids, our careers are our everything. So ten years into our friendship, we decided to make it official. Producing partners.

Even though we're still boarding, Chloe motions to a smiley flight attendant in first class. "Two champagnes please." She shimmies. Chloe shimmies a lot—when we close a deal, when a restaurant has her favorite dessert, when she dishes on her latest sexual conquest, who is usually younger and not the smartest tool in the shed. It's one of my favorite things about her.

The flight attendant's smile doesn't budge, giving the appearance that it's painted on, or that he's an android. The writer in me is obsessed with the latter. Is the android planning an elaborate hijack so he can steer the ship back to an alien planet?

Anything to keep my mind off this flight. So I tune into the saga of a J.Crew model trying to stuff an oversized roller bag into the overhead bin.

"Now she knows her bag is too big," Chloe chimes in, reading my mind. Two male flight attendants race over to help her, trying out various bag configurations like they're solving a mathematical equation.

"If that was our bag, they'd check it with the quickness," I acknowledge, salty, before adding, "And then lose it."

The robotic flight attendant brings our champagnes, still smiling. He utters no words. I'm just saying.

"We did it!" Chloe exclaims as we raise and clink our glasses.

"We have to shoot the movie first." I guzzle the bubbly with no shame. We've been trying to get this film made for almost as long as we've known each other. And we finally got the right amount of heat and white guilt to convince a Hollywood studio to give us $15 million and twenty shooting days to do it. I used to think that was a lot of money before I started to be a part of budget convos. When you're trying to cast well, pay everyone well, and shoot it well, the money goes fast. But for quiet romantic dramas where Black people are living and loving, studios have deluded themselves into believing that these types of projects, and not their tenth Marvel reboot, are the biggest risk ever. The cynic in me is on edge that at any moment, execs will hop on this plane because they remembered that they don't actually care about diversity, or they need to put the money toward another unwatchable blockbuster starring a forgettable movie star du jour. They will be watching our every move, counting every dollar, and we best not make a mistake or go over budget. And of course for us melanated, it's not just our futures on the line, but all the hopes and dreams of folks who look like us. The pressure.

"Can you celebrate for just one moment?" Chloe protests.

Sure can't. I learned a long time ago to err on the side of disappointment. To expect it really. Softens the blow when it does inevitably happen.

"Actually I do want to hold your hand," I double back to annoy her. Chloe grabs my hand to irritate me. Touché. We clasp hands like a married couple who still likes one another. It's oddly comforting.

I do all of this not because I'm afraid of a big-ass, man-made apparatus that floats in the sky. Or the serial killer lookalike across the way from us who's hacking up a lung. Or the impending hijacking attempt by the flight attendant android when Idris Elba isn't here to save us. Or for the usual go-to reason I've given Chloe and everyone who's asked: aerophobia.

The truth is… I hate flying because *he* didn't get on the plane with me that fateful day.

And I never got over it.

CHAPTER 2

SITUATIONS WILL ARISE

KYRIE

There are nearly 13,000 vacant homes in Baltimore. Think about that for a moment. Baltimore is only about 92 square miles in size with a population of about 565,000 people.

13,000 vacant homes.

The trickle-down effect is extraordinary. Crime. Fires. Lost tax revenue. Lack of affordable housing.

Loss of community.

But one of my hometown's biggest problems has become one of my biggest opportunities. I pitched the city to be their contractor of record (something they do in the advertising world) for Harlem Park, one of the neighborhoods with the most unique vacant building notices in the last year. My company isn't just rehabbing the homes, we're creating a blueprint on how to revitalize a community in partnership *with* the community. We're building confidence in Baltimore's ability to solve this problem. We're introducing a win-win workforce development program for skilled ex-offenders.

It's the busiest my company has been in its fifteen years of existence. We've got eight houses we're concurrently working on. Rocking and rolling.

And I've decided to step away for a bit.

Oscar, my second in command, doesn't get it. He reminds me of this as we walk one of the properties and inspect the progress of a roomy three-level rowhouse.

"There's bad timing and there's this," he points out like I don't realize it. Oscar's a little older than me, in his 50s, but fit like he's in his 30s. He does all that weird calisthenics at the outdoor gym in Druid Hill Park. He survived a ten-year bid for attacking the creep who assaulted his sister. Holds no bitterness or grudges. He's about the work and a cold beer when he gets off. And on most days, including this one, we're dressed like twins. Lumberjack like. Flannel shirt, jeans, Tims. Heavy belt.

"Now's your chance to audition to take this business over." Oscar hates when I talk that way. But honestly, I've been getting the itch over the last few years to do something different. Really, to get back to my first love, acting. But when I say that, most people either pity me or pray for me.

"I'm not taking over shit. This is your business and it's about to be the biggest contractor across all of Baltimore."

"Yeah we'll see. Drywall looks good. When's electrical slated to come?" I refocus on the task at hand.

"Tuesday. What if one of the guys has a… situation?"

Our guys sometimes have what we like to call situations, a catch-all term for the unique scenarios ex-offenders find themselves in. Running into a dude they had beef with on the inside and having us talk them into doing the right thing. Or missing a check-in with their PO. Or needing help adding apps to their phones.

"You'll handle it, like you handle most of them."

"And if Mayor Scott wants to drop by?"

"You'll take him on a tour of one of the properties and say all the right things."

I pat Oscar on the back. But he shakes his head, skeptical.

"You got this O," I reassure him.

But really, I'm reassuring myself.

Because what I'm about to do is absolutely nuts.

CHAPTER 3:

LIBERATION

AMAYA

The Baltimore sky beams with possibility. It's a sticky July morning. The humidity hangs so heavily in the air, you can almost see it.

I'm no longer accustomed to this type of oppressive heat. I should be more embarrassed to say that it's been too long since I've been back home. I'd visit here and there after leaving twenty years ago and never looking back. I moved my mother out to LA a few years ago, which cut down my need to return to Baltimore by about 90%. And cut down on the chances that I might run into *him*.

It was Chloe's idea for us to shoot in Charm City. "Imagine the headlines! Amaya Ellis returns home for her feature directorial debut, a gripping romantic drama about love, home, and dreams." It was quite the pitch. And she wasn't wrong. She rarely is. I did what most filmmakers do for their first film. I wrote mine loosely based on my life. And my relationship with *him*. I figure if Beyoncé could so brilliantly monetize her relationship drama, I could do the same.

The moment we touched down from our red-eye, Chloe and I sprayed some face mist, brushed our teeth, then hit the ground for jam-packed prep—department meetings, crew introductions, rehearsals. In the heat.

Sweat cascades down my face. Droplets from my chest fall onto my iPad where I scroll through my marked-up script. We're on a tech scout with my cinematographer, 1st AD, production designer and a few other crew members, touring a closed cafe for filming.

The location manager hits me with a succession of questions: Do you like the decor? Would you want additional set dressing? What about the color on the walls? We'd be able to use the furniture, do you like it?

And in kind, I respond rapid fire: Yes. Yes. No need to paint. I would only want to bring in two additional tables. Through my years of directing, I've learned that it pays to be thoughtful but decisive. And if I don't know the answer, I let them know what I need to know in order to respond or when I'll be able to get back to them.

Adorned with conversation-starting abstract art, the cafe is the perfect, quaint location for the first real date of Lyric and Dante, my main characters.

So of course, the air conditioner is stupid loud. So loud that it will be a problem for sound during filming. Everyone hops into problem solving. Can we keep it off during shooting? And burn in the hellish heat? Can we bring in our own, quieter fans? At this point, I'm decision-fatigued. And now we may have to find another location at the last minute?

As Chloe and our crew go back and forth, I find myself stealing away into the bathroom. Sitting on the toilet has become a hobby of mine. Feels like one of the only places where I can actually think. And sometimes, hide. And no, I'm not doing any business. Just sitting. Thoughts swirling around my head like flies.

Am I going to fuck up my movie?

Why is it so hot in Baltimore?

Can I rewrite this scene to take place somewhere else just in case we have to lose this location?

Is it sad that I enjoy sitting on the toilet?

Or is it sadder that I'm directing a movie about love when I myself haven't been near it since Y2K?

What is my hateful cat doing?

Since I forgot to pack my vibrator, do I order an emergency one and have it delivered to the hotel?

Is it too late to pull out of this movie so I don't completely embarrass myself?

A knock on the door startles me. "Girl, you okay? Did you have pork for breakfast again?"

"Yeah. Be out in a minute." As I take a deep breath, I slowly rise and look in the mirror. I wipe sweat from the edges of my long, beaded cornrows. Dab it from the creases of my contacted dark brown eyes. Reapply a rose-tinted gloss to my slim lips. My foundation, which perfectly matches my dewy sable skin, has melted into a sticky film. I face myself.

Will I ever be able to shake him?

He still invades my thoughts on some conqueror shit, and it's been TWENTY YEARS.

Two decades.

Almost a quarter of a century.

Do you know how much I've changed? How much I've accomplished? The life I've lived? The battles I've fought?

And I'm still hung up on a college love?

Silly, silly girl.

Enough is enough.

Slow Down, More Time will not only change my life, it will be my liberator. Once and for all.

I open the bathroom door to find Chloe waiting for me. "We have to find another location." I nod and channel my game face. Ready to do whatever it takes to make this movie and free myself.

Chloe and I are on Bookspace, an online marketplace for unique venues, trying to find another location. Our location manager is also on it, but it's too much riding on this project for us to just sit around and twiddle our anxiety.

We're at the hotel lobby bar, dressed like we're going to premieres. Me in an unassuming Prada pant suit, no shirt, no bra, and Chloe in a silky Hanifa dress. "We need to talk about the seating arrangement," I remind Chloe as we scroll through mansions, lofts, and weird rooms in even weirder houses. I rub my eyes only to look up and be accosted by the bad lighting. It's trying too hard to be moody, but instead, it's giving brothel. And the music? '80s erotic thriller. Glenn Close may just walk in.

"You need to sit next to Benji. I can't take his energy the night before shooting," I assert.

"Not tonight. He's going to want to talk to you. Make sure the studio's investment is safe." Benji is a Black executive that the studio stuck on our project to ensure we're overdelivering. He can't greenlight a film, but he can sabotage one. A power that he wields like a low-level mafia boss. He's not my cup of tea, juice, or water. He gives horrible notes, has no backbone, and talks like he's powered by A.I., a string of buzzwords—*aspirational, auteur, high concept.* I smile, laugh at his stale jokes, then sic Chloe on him.

And speak of the devil, here comes this motherfu—

"Benji!" Chloe sings his name like she's on Broadway. I fix my face and prepare to kiss ass.

"There's my favorite creative duo." He flashes his full-of-shit smile and Chloe returns hers.

"Looking dapper, Benji," I offer. This is true. Benji is easy on the eyes—tallish, gorgeous dreads, all the right facial hair and he knows what to wear on said ass.

"Gucci." He does a slow spin.

"New York Fashion Week needs you," Chloe adds. Yeah, we're laying it on thick, but… $15 million.

"So how are you feeling about tomorrow, Amaya?" Benji asks innocently, but I know it's a loaded question that I best answer correctly.

"I feel good. Ready. Excited." I feel like I'm going to throw up on his Gucci suit.

"Good, because you set the tone on set. And we need that tone to be here." He raises his hand above his head. "No pressure!"

Not long after sucking up to Benji, we're all seated, strategically, at one of those large dining room tables in a private room. It's about eight of us. All Black, which I don't take for granted. A bunch of smart, creative, and slightly neurotic, fashionably dressed Black folk coming together to make something that once lived in my imagination. It's moments like this that *almost* make all the b.s. worth it.

Benji, sitting uncomfortably close to me, leans in. "We have full faith in you and Chloe."

"Thank you," I say as I pick up my drink, readying for the *but*.

"But, I'm gonna hang around on set for a few days, make sure everything goes off smoothly."

"Great." I kick Chloe's leg who's sitting on the other side of me and didn't hear a word.

"You know, to ensure the quality meets our standards. And that everything is staying on budget and on time."

"Chloe is on top of time and budget."

"Of course she is." He doesn't trust her or us.

"I would like to make a toast to our fearless leader," Ranita, a rising young star who plays Lyric, announces with her signature dramatic flair that has made audiences fall in love with her. She reminds me of a young Margaret Avery. Regal. Effortless. Magical.

"This will be my second time working with Amaya. And each time, I learn and grow so much from the experience. I know this film is going to be amazing and I'm so grateful to be a part of it." I blush. Nothing like a Black woman complimenting you. It's like rainbows and shea butter and fairy dust. Moisturizes your self-doubt.

"Hear hear," Ranita's co-star, Tomé, chimes in, not to be outdone. "There are visionaries, and then there's Amaya." Tomé is a young brother from Detroit who steals every scene he's in. The presence of Denzel with the vulnerability of Jeffrey Wright. I am, however, pretty sure his mama named him Tommy.

Ranita and Tomé play, well, me and… *him*. But a lot better than we ever did.

Benji rises to make his remarks. "We were so excited to *champion* Amaya's feature directorial debut. We're *big fans* of hers and believe in the *universal* themes of love and ambition. Cardinal is a *filmmaker-centered* studio poised to lead the *new wave of cinema*. And we're proud to have *Slow Down, More Time* as part of our *robust* slate." Benji starts clapping and we all follow.

Chloe rises as a palate cleanser of sorts. "I want to thank Cardinal Studios, including our wonderful executive Benji, for believing in us. Amaya is not the next in filmmaking or cinema or directing. She's the now. And this project is her *Get Out*, minus the crazy white people."

"And triple the budget," Benji adds with a chuckle. The way I want to kick him under the table.

"It will have that kind of impact on the hearts of people around the world," Chloe continues without skipping a beat. "We have not seen a movie about first loves with this amount of introspection and heart and humor. We are making history and I am so proud to be on this journey with all of you, but especially my good friend and business partner, Amaya Ellis."

Well damn. Talk about setting the stage. I feel the pressure to rise amidst the applause and hollers.

"I'm not one for a lot of words, but in this moment, I just want to express my gratitude to all of you for believing in a film that showcases Black love, but isn't wrapped up into a neat bow. A film that's shot in Baltimore and that's loosely, very loosely based on my own experience. This is special. And I want to remember this feeling. And I want us to carry it onto set and throughout our 20 days together. And my hope is that this will be the gateway to more films that center us."

A joyous clinking of glasses.

Now all I have to do is deliver on the promise.

Shit.

CHAPTER 4:

BACK TO LIFE

KYRIE

It's that time of morning, where slivers of light do that dance they do. I'm not gonna lie. Shit's sexy. And peaceful. Cares fade away. I can hear my thoughts mingled with the hum of outside. And all I can think about is sharing this moment with a beautiful soul nestled in the crook of my arm, her soft ass sidled up against me. The honey smell of her hair wafting through the air. The curve of her hips—

"Want breakfast?" Shani thunderbolts into my room with the energy of a golden retriever puppy. Leaps on my bed. Boundaries be damned.

Back to life.

"I made some pancakes and they're only like half-burnt." She says as she eats one. My sixteen-year-old is many things. The spitting image of her father, but with a short natural haircut. Holder of TikTok facts. Dramatic with a capital D. A Real Housewife expert. But a cook? She burns pots boiling water.

"You made breakfast?" I ask as I reluctantly get out of bed and grab a gray tank top. I had to stop sleeping butt-ass naked a few years ago when Shani refused to knock.

"Don't be like that. I'm getting better." She pushes her asphalt pancake in my face. "Taste." I turn my head in polite refusal. She's sensitive.

"I'm sure you are. And I appreciate the offer, but I'll eat at work. Good way to meet everybody. But thank you for breakfast."

"Since I did make breakfast without you asking, I was wondering if I can spend the night at Dawn's house?" My daughter has been manipulating me since she was in the crib.

"When?"

"Tonight."

"It's a school night."

"We have a big test tomorrow and I want to study."

"You and I both know you just wanna hang out."

"Okay, that's not a bad thing. And we really do have a test. I'm sure Dawn is gonna wanna study at some point."

"Is her mother okay with it?"

"Yes."

I give my daughter the look. "Do I need to call Dawn's mother?"

"No, she's cool with it, for real. She's gonna take us to school tomorrow morning."

"Okay." I start pulling out my clothes for the day. Although I've been planning what I was going to wear for a few weeks now.

"You're wearing that?" The snide. Now I'm self-conscious as I scrutinize the white, short-sleeve button down with my favorite pair of Levi's. Clean, but not like I'm trying too hard.

"What's wrong with it?"

Shani shrugs like she never said anything.

"Sooooo, are you like, super nervous or super excited for your first day?" She rests her head on both of her knuckles and leans in like she used to do during Storytime at the local library.

I'm scared shitless. Over the years, I've had the chance to work background on the few projects that have come to Baltimore in between running my general contracting business. But now, I'm gonna be more visible as a stand-in, who literally stands in place of the lead actors for rehearsals, camera blocking, and lighting set-ups. We help the crew make sure everything is good before they start shooting.

It's a position that suits me just fine honestly, I love acting, but hate all the bullshit that comes with it. Ego trippin', lack of privacy, vultures disguised as friends. Loss of self.

I actually studied acting for a few semesters in college, but then reality caught up with me. Who did I think I was, majoring in… acting? Like bro, you're gonna need a real skill. So I switched to business. And thank God I did, especially when my daughter came along. But now that I have a good handle on everything, I felt like it was finally time to get back into the game. For the love though. I have no urge to go Hollywood.

"A little bit of both," I say, mustering a measured Dad response. Shit, if we're being honest, I act all day long. Concealing my feelings to reassure Shani that the world isn't as bad as it really is. Playing amenable Black man so I don't get shot.

"Can I visit you on set?" Shani beams. My cheerleader. She's proud of me no matter what, even when it's hard to find it in myself.

"We'll see. It's a closed set. I have to get permission." I kiss her on her forehead before she bounces out of the room.

The real reason Shani can't come to set? Because *she* will be there.

CHAPTER 5:
STEP INTO FRAME

An empty, abandoned school. Stories echo from the walls. Remnants of young joy, angst, and shenanigans. On the first day of shooting, I like to arrive early to the location, before everyone else. A ritual of mine. Helps to ground me. To dictate the energy of the shoot. To tell myself that I can do this. Because in about thirty minutes, the set will be overrun with chaos-roaring voices, on-the-move equipment, and the soundtrack of footsteps.

But now? This place has a whir and I can hear it. A rhythm. A soul. I let it wash over me and the scenes start to reveal themselves.

I walk into what will become a college eatery, think The Pit from *A Different World*. It comes alive, bustling with gossipy college kids chowing down on greasy food. In the center of the chaos, a girl and guy–Lyric and Dante–gaze into each other's eyes. Innocence drips off of them. He whispers in her ear, sneaking in a tender kiss on her earlobe. She drops her head a little as she blushes. He lifts it by her chin. Lyric and Dante become me and *him*. It's a vibey scene establishing their beginnings. *Us*, sweet and picture-book, before life took hold. I begin to remember with my body, as if it was recent.

That scares the shit out of me.

"Is it time to pray?" Chloe, a Buddhist who prays like a storefront Baptist preacher and loves a First Lady hat, stumbles in. I snap out of the scene, gratefully. But I'm shooketh for a beat.

Praying is a ritual of ours. We pray away demonic spirits—the spirit of over time, over budget, and over acting. And I throw in an extra one today: over feeling.

"Ready?" Chloe holds up her palms. I grab them.

Yes, yes I am. We bow our heads.

• • ● • •

"Don't you want more out of life than this?" Ranita delivers her line with such elegance that I have to swallow my emotion during rehearsal. Even Tomé softens and opens in a beautiful way. It's a scene toward the end of their relationship where Lyric finally convinces Dante to move with her to Los Angeles. Or so she thinks.

"That's a cut on rehearsal," my 1st AD, Yusef, announces. I want to melt into the floor. We're on our second scene of the day, and it already has been an exercise in keeping my emotional shit together. The way I was transported to my twenty-year-old self delivering that same line to *him*.

But with zero elegance. And he didn't soften. I wish I could have called "cut" then and adjusted our performances.

While the actors go off to hair and makeup, I retreat to video village to gather myself. I slump in the director's chair with my name on it that's stationed in front of two monitors, one for each camera.

I inhale and exhale deep-ass yoga breaths. I had to know that writing and then directing a film "loosely based" on the biggest love and heartbreak of my life, would stir up some… feelings. But not like this.

"Kinera has some new makeup ideas she wants to run by you." Chloe plops into her named chair, followed by her tagalong, Benji, whose chair reads "Guest." I straighten up, start scrolling the script on my iPad. "You alright?" she whispers, sensing something, but I will not let on. Not with Benji there.

"If Ranita and Tomé keep doing what they did in rehearsal, we've got an award winner on our hands," I say in Benji's language.

Chloe shimmies. "That's what I'm talking about."

"Good to hear," Benji responds. "We'll see how that translates to filming." I don't need his pessimism. I have enough of my own.

"Did I hear something about a location falling through?"

Chloe and I exchange looks. Here we go.

"We're on it," she shoots back quickly.

"Good, because at the last look at the budget, it would basically have to be free."

We both nod. And by the grace of God, he gets a call that forces him to step away. And immediately, Chloe turns to me.

"So I didn't want to say it while our friend was here, but we are gonna need that location for free. The leads we did have aren't working out. Oh, and I worry that Kinera is gonna have our entire cast looking like Tammy Faye Bakker."

I interrupt that one. "I thought Zena recommended her."

"She did, but homegirl is trying to turn our film into a horror through makeup."

And so the problems begin. "Go through our database and check availability on our top rated Makeup Department Heads. Just so we know what we're working with. In the meantime, I'll talk to her. We'll give her a couple of days and then make a decision."

"Aye aye, captain."

Benji reappears like a ghost. Sits down and gets comfortable.

So I start watching the monitors to avoid conversation with our babysitter. My cinematographer, Zena, is testing lighting and layering the frame with so much intention and depth. It's why I prefer working with women DPs, their lensing tends to have a unique tenderness.

The woman who's acting as Ranita's stand-in is stunning. She's peering directly into the camera as Zena and our gaffer adjust lighting. There's a sadness to her that I feel so very deeply.

As I swim in those feelings, *he* steps into frame.

And I fucking lose it.

My breathing quickens and I can't catch it.

Him.

The one.

Who I left.

Who didn't come with me.

Who "inspired" this movie.

Who I think about damn near daily.

Him.

"Okay, stand-in. He's nice looking. What's his name?" Chloe inquires.

"Wow, he does pop on screen," Benji adds.

I say nothing because I can't. Instead I just stare at his face, so full and satisfying and smug in the frame. It's like he wants me to gaze into his beautifully round eyes that are accentuated by the longest, sexiest eyelashes. Damn *him*!

"Amaya!" Apparently this is the third time Chloe has tried to get my attention.

"Huh? What?"

"Zena wants you on set. She has a question."

I nod.

On set.

Near *him.*

Okay.

Yep.

I can do that.

Except I don't move. Chloe's hella concerned. Benji is confused. Chloe basically pushes me out of my chair. And escorts me like a bailiff.

"Girl, are you okay? Are you constipated?"

Why she always defers to my gastrointestinal system is beyond me.

Olivia, our costume designer, accosts me. "There she is. What do you think about this dress for Lyric for the first date scene?"

"Uh. I like it. I think. I mean. Should it be a little dressier or more casual? I don't know." This mofo has me discombobulated. And now, watching me babble, Chloe's freaking out. She cracks her knuckles, the opposite of shimmying. She answers Olivia for me, then sends her on her way.

"Okay, what is going on?" She demands an answer.

I pull her aside, and look around like I'm about to reveal national security secrets.

"I need you to fire the stand-in."

"The cutie? Why?"

"Because."

"Did you smoke this morning?"

"It's *him.*"

Chloe's head falls back like it's going to fall off. *"Him, him?"*

I nod, still mired in disbelief. "And I'm already messed up. I can't think or make a simple decision.

"Well no shit. You were talking gibberish to Olivia." Chloe takes a deep breath. Luckily she thrives in fires like this.

"Give me until the end of the day. We need him right now and have no time to slow down. And I have to do it on the low so Benji doesn't catch wind. Can you hang on until then?"

I nod, very unconvincingly as we finally reach the set.

He turns around and there years between us, but only a few feet right now. So much left unsaid between us, but now, no words uttered. You can see my chest rise and fall as I try to breathe through it.

I turn toward Chloe and apologize with my eyes. Because I go and do some erratic shit. As Zena and her gaffer rejig some lights, I march up to Kyrie and say, "You have a minute? I have some notes."

Chloe is horrified, knuckle cracking on ten.

I don't wait for his response. I don't waste time clocking any weird looks I may be receiving because I just told a stand-in that I have notes. I just walk into the hallway and out the door.

Outside, there's a line of trucks with a security guard watching the comings and goings. A bunch of crew adhere drapes to the windows while preparing to move our big-ass camera rig.

I keep walking, maneuvering around machinery, hopping over wires, until I find a small nook two doors down from the school. I face *him*, but I don't face *him*. I don't look at *him*.

He speaks first. "Good to see you Amaya," he says like we saw each other at a social gathering earlier in the year.

Be fucking for real.

"What are you doing here?"

"Working."

"Bullshit."

Kyrie smiles, flashing those dimples that I used to dig my fingers in. And this Negro has the nerve to look BET-TER than he did twenty years ago. And taller? Fitter! Finer! Life is unfair.

"You're a piece of work, you know that? Are you trying to sabotage me?"

"You know me better than that."

"Do I?"

Kyrie takes a slow, methodical step towards me. And I hippity hop the fuck back. Still, I can smell *him*, a mix of clove, orange, and potent masculinity. I'm crashing out as my niece likes to say.

"Beyond this salt and pepper beard, I'm still the same Kyrie." He looks at me like he remembers me. Us. Like nothing in between matters. Like this is the most important moment. Like we are the most important thing.

And I finally allow myself to look at *him*. Really look at *him*. Eyes that issue heavenly invites. Lips, thick, soft, defined. Beckoning. The beard he so slyly pointed out? Perfectly groomed and speckled. Punctuating a godly goatee. It's a fucking problem. Why am I cursing so much? See! This is what he does. Disarms the mess out of me.

"You didn't answer my question." I fold my arms like a sassy teen.

"I'm here because it's a great opportunity."

This is that bullshit, I begin to walk off, but he ever so gently, lovingly actually, grabs my arm and pulls me back into whatever the hell this is.

"And I wanted to see you. You got me there."

There are places I would like to have him as my eyes, completely on their own volition, linger around the base of his neck, working their way down the ripples in his chest and before I get to what used to be my throne—

I resume control. "Well, you've done that. This will be your first and last day," I say devoid of emotion. Proud of myself.

"Sorry to hear that. You know, all I've ever wanted was for you to win."

Another standoff. But this one, I walk away from.

Again.

He will not ruin this for me.

I will not let *him*.

CHAPTER 6:
FIRE AND FEAR

KYRIE

Memory is a funny thing. It's both fixed and fluid. Real and imaginary. Safe and utterly dangerous. I fidget in bed while flashes of Amaya haunt me.

Her eyes, full of fire and fear.

I didn't know what to expect when she saw me. I knew it wouldn't be a rosy reunion. But damn, to pull me aside while I'm working like I was doing something wrong?

Her lips, glossy and commanding.

If she wasn't directing this movie, I would have still submitted for the stand-in position. It's a great opportunity. I wasn't lying to her when I said that. For her to think that I want to sabotage her movie is mad offensive. That's what she thinks of me after all these years?

Selfishly, I guess that's what I wanted to know. Has she thought about me?

Amaya was the one who got away.

And I wanted to know how far her heart has gone.

Because mine still beats for *her*. It always has.

I loved Shani's mother, but it was a different love. A grown up, practical love. That I learned so much from.

But Amaya and I's love was full of hope. It was raw, alive.

How her cleavage played peekaboo under her tank top.

And I let her get on that plane without me.

The biggest mistake of my life.

She's more confident. Comfortable in her skin. Grown woman shit. Sexy as hell. Damn. I feel my shit swelling. I slide my hand down my boxers and grab it with the intensity I used to grab her thighs with. I start to stroke it slowly at first. That's how I like to enter the palace, gently but confidently. Appreciating my welcome. Just as I begin to grip faster–

My phone buzzes. Shit! Completely kills the vibe I got going on. It's Lisa, the mother of Dawn, Shani's friend. She's over her house for a sleepover.

Back to life.

"Hey Lisa, everything okay?" My hand still on that rock.

Everything is not okay.

··●··

"She's always talking shit and then she got in my face," Shani claims, worked up in the passenger seat, rocking a bruise over her left eye and a ripped tee from one of those cheap online knockoff stores.

"You told me it was going to be just you and Tiesha sleeping over at Dawn's." This girl likes to leave out important details.

"I can't control who Dawn has at her house." As she sucks her teeth, she knows she's gone too far. I don't even need to deliver the Black parent have-you-lost-your-mind look. She's got *some* sense. But it's moments like this where I wish I didn't have to do parenthood alone. Shani's mother died in a car accident when she was five. Drunk driver. I grieved while learning how to do my daughter's hair, buying grocery store cookies for her class, and fumbling my way through the period talk.

"I didn't know Brenda's bitch ass was gonna be there."

"Enough with the cursing."

"She started calling Nia all these names and you know I don't play about my girlfriend."

"I thought you and Jabari were together." My daughter identifies as pansexual. I had to look it up. Basically she's just equal opportunity. But she's also a heartbreaker.

"Dad, that was last month. Like keep up."

"You know you're grounded for the next few days, right?"

"I was defending myself and my girl."

"You and Brenda have had beef since y'all were freshmen. You've been waiting for an excuse to beat her ass. I have a 4:30 am call time. I had to get out of bed, disrupt… my life, to pick you up because you were trying to prove a point?"

"I wasn't proving a point. I was fighting for love!"

I can only shake my head at her passion.

Wishing I had half of it when I was her age.

Because maybe if I did, Amaya would remember me differently.

But let my daughter tell it, sometimes you gotta make people know that you're for real.

And that's what I intend to do.

CHAPTER 7

MEET CUTE

THEM: 1998

Professor Randall thought that having class in the musty basement of Banneker Hall at Morgan State made learning feel more urgent. And thus, the scenes performed by her budding thespians, more authentic.

But to her students, the makeshift classroom was just hot and musty. To the point that eighteen-year-old Amaya was sweating through her pink Limited halter top, unflattering rings under her arms that she worked hard to hide. Thank God her hair was in box braids or her perm would be half bush by now.

"Today we're looking at one of my favorite types of scenes, 'The Meet Cute'." Professor Randall clasps her hands like a schoolgirl.

"Does anyone know what a meet cute is?" Professor Randall adjusts her glasses and her wig.

"I could use some cute meat right about now," a student murmurs to giggles. But Amaya doesn't laugh. She's too busy being self-conscious. She took an acting class because she wants to be a great director. But she dreads every single session, especially when she has to perform. She tries to offset her horrible acting with her deep knowledge of all things film. So, she raises her hand.

"A meet cute is when two people meet for the first time, usually in a fun or weird way, but they end up in the movie together."

Professor Randall nods gleefully. "Precisely, Amaya. I'm going to pair the class up and give each duo a scene from a classic romance movie."

Horrific is the only way to describe the pit in Amaya's stomach as Professor Randall assigns couples. So much so that she barely notices nineteen-year-old Kyrie, tall, dark, and dumb fine, approach her.

"I think we're partners." Amaya's gaze lifts, starting from Kyrie's Tims to the top of his Orioles fitted cap. In between? Baggy jeans that don't hide a bulge. A v-neck white tee that exposes a chest so firm, so chocolate. She wants to lick it. Every ounce of him is glorious. And a panty-wetting smile to match? He grabs a chair, flips it backwards and straddles it. He is uncomfortably close to her.

"You ever heard of this movie, *Claudine*?" he asks while reviewing their scene. Amaya lights up.

"Diahann Carroll and James Earl Jones. Performances to die for. Diahann was actually nominated for an Oscar, but of course she didn't win. And to this day we've never had a Black woman win an Academy Award for Best Actress. Can you believe that? The film's directed by John Berry, a white guy, who apparently was blacklisted by Hollywood for being a communist. But it didn't completely derail his career, he actually directed this after said blackball. I love movies. I want to be a director. I'm only here to get better at directing."

After Amaya vomits her encyclopedia knowledge, Kyrie nods. Then adds, "Darth Vader. Okay!"

A very awkward beat between these two.

"You want to just say the words first?" Amaya cuts through it. She read a book about directing that suggested reading a scene aloud first is a great way to start rehearsal.

"Sure, why not." Kyrie gets up, all 6'4" of him. Amaya's head ascends like she's taking in a skyscraper.

He takes a deep breath, then with the presence of James Earl Jones, he takes center stage:

RUPERT: "How are you today?"

Amaya's so mesmerized by his delivery of the benign line that she misses her cue.

"Your turn," Kyrie patiently prompts her.

"Oh, right."

CLAUDINE: "Just fine. How are you?"

Amaya has the right to be self-conscious. She's awful. Overdoing it. Not at all believable or human.

Kyrie thinks it's cute. He grins at her attempt.

RUPERT: "Oh, just fine. Say, uh, tell the man that, uh…Tell the man that I'm not taking this one."

CLAUDINE: "Oh, lord. That's sure gon' make him mad."

Amaya's ears cringe hearing herself. Her rendition of *gon'* got stuck at the roof of her mouth. Frustration takes over. "I'm not good at this. You should find another partner."

"Don't try to act. Just be in it. With me." Kyrie gently taps Amaya's shoulder. A current with a power that she can't quantify runs through her body.

Amaya leans into the feeling. Of being in it. With him.

RUPERT: "Yeah, I guess so. You do look fine today. 'Course you look fine all the time. You know, I know, I'm just an ugly old smelly old garbage man. But you see me all cleaned up, you won't believe your eyes. Say, you know, I've been studyin' on taking you out for a long time. What about that, girl?"

Chile… Amaya is in it.

"Yes."

Kyrie looks down at the scene. "I don't think that's your line."

Amaya is so in it that she says what she would naturally say. Yes.

"Oh, right."

CLAUDINE: "No, I don't think so."

RUPERT: "Oh, you don't want me to beg ya, do you baby?"

CLAUDINE: "No."

"See, you're getting the hang of it."

She blushes. "You're really good."

Now he blushes.

Afterward, as Amaya packs up her things, Kyrie, now not in character, nervously asks, "Do you want to grab lunch at the Caf and talk about acting and maybe you can teach me about directing? Only if you want to." He glances away briefly, a tinge of embarrassment.

"I would love to." Amaya accepts with curious eyes and fresh desire.

And so it begins.

CHAPTER 8:
A KIND OF FOREPLAY

AMAYA

Building a schedule for a movie is a delicate dance, a calculated equation. So many factors have to be considered: location availability, cast schedules, length of each scene. And once you finally figure out the complicated puzzle, you don't want to mess with it.

I pay Yusef, my 1st AD, a visit at the production offices to do just that. Chloe needed more time to get rid of Kyrie, something about retaliation, probable cause, and avoiding legal action, so I had to take matters into my own antsy hands.

"Just so I understand, you want to move any scenes with Tomé to the end of the schedule?" Yusef is rightfully confused.

"Yes. I want to continue to build the chemistry between Ranita and Tomé behind the scenes. So that when they are on screen together, it lights up like the 4th of July." I'm not a great liar and an even worse actor, but I'm desperate.

"But you also don't want to do scenes with just Tomé and no Ranita?" Yusef continues to try to understand. What I'm proposing is nonsensical. But it's necessary.

"Changes like this so late in the game often come at a cost." He adds.

I was hoping that wouldn't be the case. But as long as I've been working in this business, I should know better.

"We can't afford to go over budget." This is my way of saying do it if there's a little wiggle room in the budget, knowing good and well that there is no wiggle room in the budget. He will have to pull off a miracle.

Yusef analyzes his *Minority Report* corkboard that's wallpapered with blueprints, maps, and photo printouts. He studies the shooting schedule, his chin resting in his hand. Lots of head shaking. He walks away and then back to it. I dare not disturb him.

"I'll have to take a closer look."

"Of course."

"If you need it for your process…" He's giving me an out before he fiddles with the tightly laid schedule.

"I do. I really do. Thanks, Yusef. Appreciate you."

And that's how I've managed to avoid Kyrie all week. I don't know exactly how he made it work, but Yusef adjusted the schedule so that we shot scenes without Tomé, and therefore had no need for Kyrie, his stand-in.

Until today.

It was the only way I was going to focus and find my zone. I figured once I established my footing, Chloe would be able to get rid of *him*. And I have found my footing.

I'm back to my decisive self. Blocking like a beast. Crafting inspired shots with Zena. The studio is pleased with the dailies–the footage that's distributed from each day's shoot. So I have to keep my eyes on the prize. There's no room for error.

But today? Today we're shooting the steamy, loving-in-the-shower scene. The first time Lyric and Dante actually have sex. It begins with a scene in a hotel room that Dante has refashioned with romance overload: rose petals, candles, minibox playing love jams.

Personally, it's been years since I've experienced any semblance of romance and it's been close to half of a presidential term since I got dicked down. I'm about to combust.

"Is it too dark? Should they put up more lighting?" Oh and Benji is here. All day. Breathing down my neck. In an Armani suit. He's been popping in and out the last few days because he was in the middle of a bidding war for a sci-fi, action, thriller, horror romance starring Timothée Chalamet. His studio won and now he's back giving bad notes and thinking he's hot shit.

"The scene is supposed to be moody. Intimate. A kind of foreplay," I respond, assuming he doesn't know jack shit about anything remotely related to romance.

"What about putting a lamp in the corner?" The stupidest idea I've heard from him yet.

"That's interesting. I'll talk to Zena about it." I use that as an excuse to get the hell out of there.

As I walk the long way towards the set, there's Kyrie laughing with Hair and Makeup, departments who always find a nook in the cut to set up for touch ups and last looks. I find myself zooming in on him for a moment. The tilt of his head. The curve of his top lip. He approaches and I snap out of it. He will not draw me in again.

But first I need to pass by *him*. Through a tight hallway. I affix myself to the wall behind me so I don't accidentally brush up against him or his thang.

He nods respectfully, which pisses me off. He's still here and has the nerve to be professional.

After that close call, it's time for the shower scene. We're filming it in a shower that's built on a soundstage so that we can shoot it from all sides. First up is a closed rehearsal with Ranita and Tomé. Because it's such an intimate scene, I only allow the actors, my DP, the intimacy coordinator, and the stand-ins to watch.

When I shoot love scenes, I explore a loose choreography with the actors that feels natural to them. Sometimes I need to employ some connection exercises to help the actors bond, but the chemistry between Ranita and Tomé is *Love Jones* level.

This is my first time working in front of *him*. I can feel his eyes and judgement on my back as I walk Ranita and Tomé through the scene.

"Remember this is, uh… uh. Sorry. This scene is you know, good. Has some good things in it. Important things. Story points." The actors stare at me, bewildered at my choppy direction. I give myself a quick pep talk in my head: STOP BEING A SILLY BITCH. I clear the nerves in my throat. Push through. "It's the first time they've been together. And it's lovemaking. Tender. Intentional. A lot of restraint. Yearning. Settling in."

"My specialty," Tomé inappropriately shares.

"So I was thinking you two could start with just taking each other in. Every detail. Even the ones you are being reintroduced to." Ranita and Tomé begin to embody my blocking. "Then your hands begin to slowly travel, explore, caress." I circle them, admiring their gentleness with one another while considering potential camera placements and angles. I catch Kyrie in my eyeshot, seemingly captivated. I whip pan my head back to the cast and finish walking them through the scene.

As we wrap rehearsal, I glance over to see Kyrie taking notes. Being serious about this and his job. The gall. As I walk past, he politely stops me.

"Quick question, how far do you want me and Tina to go?" Tina is Ranita's stunning stand-in. I'm thrown off by how much he wants to actually do a good job.

"Just really want you two to mime action, nothing more."

"Got it, thanks. And it looks like it's going to be a beautiful scene."

His sincerity wraps around me like a blanket.

"Thank you." He offers a smile before going off to rehearse with Tina.

I head back to video village, only to find it empty and Kyrie dead center of the frame of A monitor, shirtless. His eyes lowered. None of the words – built, chiseled, muscled, broad – can describe the absolute work of art that is his upper body. For a brief moment, he looks into the camera, dead at me. Radiating.

He… is… a… star.

"Amaya." Chloe steps in front of me like a momma who had to leave work because her child was acting up in school. "You need to pull it together."

"I need Kyrie to be gone."

"I'm working on it, but until then, you can't be caught up in the rapture like Anita Baker."

Too late.

CHAPTER 9

HOW MUCH DO I LOVE THEE?

THEM: 2000

These two found creating together very, very sexy. So they did it, ahem, created, all the time. Today, they're practicing a monologue for Kyrie to perform in Morgan's variety show. Amaya wrote and is directing the piece about a young man who's in love with his best friend, but she doesn't know it. It's funny, heartfelt, and showcases all of their talents well.

"Let's start from the top, and this time, consider breaking the fourth wall. What would it look like if you interacted with the audience?" At this stage in her artistic journey, Amaya loved to push the envelope.

Kyrie, not so much. "Yo, your mind is wild. Love that about you." Kyrie steals a quick kiss. "I just don't want to confuse the audience though."

"I hear that. So maybe we have to establish at the start of the piece that we're going to be breaking the fourth wall. Let's just try it."

Kyrie's hesitant, but he goes along with it. He always goes along with Amaya's ideas and ambitions. He grounds himself, then begins.

"How much do I love thee? Let me count the ways. Nah, nah. Y'all would be here all day." They're in an empty auditorium so Kyrie hops off the stage and sits in one of the chairs to talk to an invisible audience member. "Sometimes I just want to thank her Momma. That's how fine she is." Amaya motions for him to get up and walk down the aisle. She follows a tad too closely behind him.

Kyrie's on the move. "But she's smart too. Like some kind of genius." He stops walking, turns toward Amaya. "This feels like it's too much."

Amaya considers. "Okay, maybe we don't start here. Maybe we end here."

"I'm not feeling it, A. Let's go back to your original direction on stage. You came up with some amazing movement and blocking. Classic material." He caresses her arms.

She knows he's right. "Thank you for indulging me."

"Always." He dips her. They share a laugh and then he hops on the stage.

They get back to work. Back to creating. Back to loving.

CHAPTER 10

SHOULDA, WOULDA, COULDA

KYRIE

Melba's is an around-the-way spot with heavy pours, throw-back decor – think mirrored wall – and a soundtrack with joints like Luther's "Never Too Much." Strictly for the thirty and up crew. So yes, I've been coming here for fifteen years. While sipping on bourbon, I check Shani's location on Life360 to make sure she's at her cousin's house like she's supposed to be. I hate feeling like the Feds, but this is the world we live in. And Shani can be slick when she wants. Then I navigate over to Amaya's IG page. It's creep behavior, but being around her has stirred up way more shit than I expected. One, how unassumingly beautiful she is. And always has been. Two, how much her talent has grown and matured. And three, how badly I fumbled *her*.

"Okay Denzel!" My homeboy Bryant always has to make an entrance.

"Yo, are you wearing a cowboy hat?"

"That cowboy shit is in right now. I'm out here lasso-ing honeys." Bryant does a very bad rodeo impression before plopping down on a bar stool.

"But enough about my fashion savvy, what's up with the movie?"

"Being back on set feels good. And weird. And like I may have been missing out all these years. I love watching Amaya block scenes and give direction. It's inspiring watching the young actors do their thing. I feel like I'm back in an immersive school so I'm soaking everything up."

"Yeah, your ass should have never quit acting. But we already know that. Get to the good part. What happened when Amaya saw your ass?"

"It's been rocky."

"Of course it has. You basically left her at the altar."

Bryant winks at a Brickhouse who just walked in.

"She still seems pretty upset about it."

"You know women don't get over shit like that. Even if they get back with you, they're always gonna remember and make sure you know that they remember."

Bryant and I have been friends since high school. Held each other down through the best and worst of life. Most recently, Bryant's divorce from a chick half his age who walked away with half his money and most of his pride. I have never seen a man cry as much as he did. He knew he married her for all the wrong reasons. Now he's in the streets and giving out relationship advice.

"She did great without me," I try to justify. "Maybe I did her a favor."

"Women don't find that pity shit sexy."

That makes me guzzle the remainder of my drink.

"What's your plan?"

And therein lies the problem. I don't have one beyond keep my head down, finish the shoot and return to my life.

Make believe isn't real.

CHAPTER 11

TAKE A RIDE IN MY TAHOE

AMAYA

"Shorty you phat, make me wanna hit that."
Baltimore club music blasts from six-foot speakers in the corners of the spot. Sometimes I think you gotta be from here to understand how poetic the genre is. And compelling. The way the frenetic beats blackmail me to shake my ass, girl. It's remarkable.

"I'm tryna gooo, take a ride in my Tahoe."
We're in the back room of Melba's Place, where all the action is. And by action, I mean a dancefloor packed with bodies bumping up against bodies. Melba's is a spot I've only been to a few times back in the day because it was for the grown and sexy. I was neither at the time. And I'm barely them now.

But the sisters in here tonight have been grown. Been sexy. And are acutely unashamed. They are letting it all hang out–titties, rolls, thighs, asses–and dare you to say something. Baltimore been body positive.

Yet here I am looking like a straight square in a long, loose summer dress that I got from a boutique for unemployed white women on Melrose, revealing nothing but my insecurities.

"I heard she got caught stealing on the job." That's Jazzy, a friend from high school who was the queen of Poly and still is. She knows everything about everyone we graduated with. She's married to the head of the football team. Hates him, but will never leave.

We're all shouting.

After wrapping my first week of filming, I would have preferred a bottle of Riesling, a hot bath, and a good cry. It was Chloe who talked me into coming and hanging with my girls from back in the day. Partly to help me get the rhythm of the city into my bones again. But also, because homebody has become part of my identity and not in a good way.

"Have you ever met Michael B. Jordan? The way I would suck the sk–." And that's Bea, AKA Adina Howard Jr. Three children. Three fathers. All of them fine. All of them worship the ground she struts on. I wish I had an ounce of whatever that is.

"Worked with him once when he made an appearance on a show I was directing. Cool guy. Young." I roll my shoulders to the music trying to be as cool as my life sounds.

"What about Idris?" Jazzy counters.

"I wish."

"So what actors are you dating, then?" Chianti is confused on why it seems like I haven't bagged a rich celebrity. Sometimes I wonder the same thing. I've been single for so long, it is damn near my sexual orientation. And if I was going to tolerate the Hunger Games-esque nature of modern dating, wealth would be a nice consolation prize.

"I don't like to mix business with pleasure." It sounds ridiculous coming out of my mouth. Truth is, I'm just an *Essence* article. I spent the last twenty years building my career and didn't prioritize much else outside of me and Chloe's friendship. There have been suitors here and there but none more interesting than the characters I have written.

"Let me find out you ain't fucking." Jazzy laughs, dripping with judgement. All of which I deserve. It's sad. Uncalled for. So I gander around at the men in Melba's. Maybe I can settle for one for the night. There's a cat daddy whose gold tooth sparkles when he smiles. No. A big ole linebacker bopping his head. Maybe. A lanky guy dancing for his life. Absolutely not.

As I continue my scan, we see each other at the same time. He pauses his steps. His eyes smile first.

It goes MOS like in the movies. No sound.

And everyone disappears like in the fairy tales.

It's just me and *him*.

Everything melts away. No regrets. No expectations. No mistakes.

Only now.

Pure, unadulterated desire.

All of a sudden, I'm hot as shit. Burning up. Like I'm back in Professor Randall's stank basement classroom.

He walks toward me.

And for the first time in a long time, I don't turn away. I start walking towards him too.

We meet in the center of the dancefloor, under a perfectly positioned purple light. He lifts my chin and burrows into my soul, seemingly wanting to know, understand, feel every inch of me.

Goddamn.

He leans down and all I want to do is bite his face. Our lips are about to dance, when someone bumps the shit out of him. And we're thrown back into reality. A jammed dancefloor. He says something that I can't hear over the music.

"If it's your birthday make some noise…"

So he whispers in my ear, "Do you wanna get out of here?"

Yes. I wave goodbye to my homegirls who clap dramatically for me, a mix of happy, about time, and thank God.

Hell yes.

Now.

CHAPTER 12

THE PINNACLE OF ROMANCE

KYRIE

"I sat in the theater for another thirty minutes after the movie ended."

"Same!" Amaya lights up with a youthful glee, like we're back in college.

"The ushers had to come and get me, like bruh, it's time to go."

We ended up at Never on Sunday, a dependable and iconic Bmore hole in the wall, sharing a cheesesteak like we're back at Morgan. No frills. Sitting across from one another, in our own world. It's kinda perfect.

"I just think that Ryan Coogler is one of the smartest directors of our generation. The projects he selects, goes after, puts together… perfection. He inspires me."

"What else inspires you?" I want to know every single thing about *her*. What she likes to eat for breakfast. Her favorite book. Flats or drums. The cameras she prefers to shoot on.

Has she thought about me?

Amaya glances down for a beat, contemplative, then to the sky, moved. "It's usually the little things, you know? The way that the light shines through tree branches. The rhythm of drums playing in Leimert Park in LA. The convo between two O.G.s at the DMV."

"Life."

"Yeah, life." A moment between us. Connection taking hold.

"I missed these," Amaya comments, eyes closed, while savoring her half of the greasy sandwich. Strictly off impulse, I gently use my thumb to wipe the mozzarella cheese hanging from her lip. She jerks her head back.

"Sorry, you–"

"Did you get it all?"

I smile, remembering that she can be a sloppy eater when she really likes something.

"I got it." She licks her lips and keeps grubbing. And I keep going. "I'm so proud of you, Amaya. For real. Every time I see your name on a television episode that you've written or directed, I'm cheesing from ear to ear. And it's always my favorite episode of the season."

"You're just saying that."

"I don't need to do that." She studies me for a beat, trying to see if I'm full of shit.

"Okay, what is your favorite episode of mine that I directed?" I smile at the challenge. Take my time to mess with her.

"It's a tie between your second episode of *The Bear*, 'cause you've directed two for that show so far, right? And your episode of *Insecure*. You were in your bag with that one. Every frame was a portrait."

She clenches her lips, cocks her head to the side. She didn't expect all of that. And that is how you silence any doubt about your sincerity.

"You've been following my career."

"I have, and it's been a joy to watch."

She lets a smile slip. "That shoot for *The Bear* was a hard one," she offers. "But I learned the magic of compression socks. Life savers."

"Well, you made it look easy." I'm clearly on a streak, so no stopping now. "I got to read the script. Took me back."

"It's only loosely based on… us." She seems a little embarrassed.

"It was nice reliving some of… our moments. The script is special. Truly."

"Thank you," she replies with a tint of sadness.

"I did have a question about the ending."

"What about it?" She places her cheesesteak down on the greased-up aluminum foil.

"Usually with romance, there's a happy ending." I begin to tread a little more lightly.

"That's rom-coms. This is a romantic drama. A happy ending for this story isn't honest."

Her eyes are down so I can't read them. But her hands fidget over her sandwich before she picks it back up.

"But you can choose any ending that you want. That's the beauty of the form."

"And I chose the one that was real."

Regret usually creeps up my back, subtly, while I'm at a site or rewatching *The Sopranos*. But this gust of regret is a new feeling. A painful one.

"Since we're asking questions, when did you start acting again?" She's challenging me. Great scenes have a turn in them, a shift in circumstances or in a character's emotional state. This is the turn in our scene.

"Been doing stuff here and there, but this is kinda like my debut back."

"Why this project?" She's trying to keep her cool, but I can tell she's in her feelings.

"Well, not many productions come here. Seemed like a great project when I first read about it on the casting website and then when I learned you were doing it, it was a no-brainer."

"You thought it would be a good idea to surprise me like that?"

"No. But it was a risk worth taking."

"Why?"

I either come clean now or I let her pass me by like I did last time.

"Because I wanted to know if there was still something here, between us. I never stopped thinking about you or rooting for you. Every day I wonder what my life would be like if I would have gotten on that plane with you."

Exhale for both of us.

She's not done.

"Why did you stop acting in the first place? It was your dream." That one makes me drop my head in a twinge of shame.

"The truth?"

She cocks her head at the obvious.

"I didn't think I'd be good enough to make a real living out of it." There I said it. I've uttered versions of this in the past to family and friends. But never this clearly. And never to *her*.

She scoops up more meat on her sandwich to avoid eye contact.

"That's very honest of you."

"Learned it in therapy."

Amaya shakes her head, amused.

"What?"

"Did you also learn all the right things to say?"

"You like what I'm saying?"

"I didn't say that."

Another moment between us. This one full of what-ifs.

And I'm tired of what-ifs. It's how I've lived my life since that day I didn't show up at the airport, effectively walking away from her and from acting. Safe is overrated. Fear is a bitch.

Maybe because I have the house to myself and feel like a teenager whose parents are out of town. Maybe because if

I don't ask now, I may never. Maybe because I haven't been this intellectually, emotionally, and physically stimulated since Obama's first inauguration. Maybe because Shani and I deep cleaned the house to '90s R&B last weekend. Maybe because the long-ass dress she has on only makes me imagine more what's underneath. Maybe because even with cheese dangling from her face, Amaya's the sexiest woman I have ever sat across. Fuck it.

"Do you want to come over?"

CHAPTER 13

A WHOLE VIBE.
A WHOLE PROBLEM.

AMAYA

Maybe I am just super horny. Or lonely. Or on a high because I finished the first week of filming for my first movie. Or because the way he gushed over my work made me gushy. Or maybe Kyrie is just fine and big and strong and tonight I want fine and big and strong.

So here I am, on a not-so-innocent tour of Kyrie's gutted and gorgeous Bolton Hill brownstone. I feel like one of Marcus Graham's prey in the movie *Boomerang*. In my twenties, this four-walled property alone would have me dropping the panties. He always did have taste. Vintage furniture reupholstered to marry modern with classic. Stunning fixtures and wall colors. Classic books and records scattered about. Bold, Black art covers the walls. He runs down the aesthetic and history of each artist. And normally, I'd be tuned in, but all I can concentrate on is the slight hug of his jeans around his very firm ass. I would love to film here. I would love to do other things here.

"Glass of wine?" he asks, like he doesn't know what he's doing.

"I like a sweet white."

"I have a sweet white."

Of course he does. We sit on his dark brown leather couch, enjoying our wine and his playlist of Sir, Alex Isley, and Syd.

A whole vibe. A whole problem.

"So you're like a renaissance man, huh?" Now I sound like I'm in *Boomerang.*

"I've always been an artsy cat, you know that."

"People change."

"Not as much as we think they do."

Who is this dude? "What do you want?" I ask point blank. That was a mistake because he puts his glass down. Does the same with mine. Places his big hands on my thighs and pulls me close to *him.* So very close to *him.*

And whispers in my ear, "To taste you."

So... I let *him.*

Who am I to deny sweet goodness to a parched, strong-handed man? He starts by sweetly kissing my forehead. Then each eye. Each cheek. A tasty lick of my lips. The base of my neck. Each shoulder. He waits for a nod from me before unbuttoning my dress like it's his life's work. He thumbs my nipples like he's serenading me with a guitar. Then he butterflies them with such passion, such precision. I wrap my legs around his waist and grind my hips against his. He wets his fingers then slips them down my panties and instantly caresses that soft spot. Sucks his finger.

"Mmmm." He sits me up on the sofa, gets on his knees, and that's when I stop him. "We need to keep this between us, okay?"

He nods quickly. And I accept that like he's just been sworn in.

"Tell me how you like it." I look down at him. His eyes plead. I'm not used to being asked.

"Slower." He's even more turned on as he follows my directions.

"Like that? Direct me."

"Just. Like. That."

"Yes, director. You taste like ice cream." He's a liar, but I love it, especially him addressing me like we're on set. My eyes roll back in pleasure. I grip his vintage table behind me with one hand, and his head with the other.

"I want you to cum." He eggs me on. And I allow myself to feel every single sensation pulsing through my body. Down my body. In my body. Across my body.

"Kyrie. Oh my God. Kyrie." I bite the shit out of my own lip as I push his face deeper between my thighs until I orgasm like an Olympic champion.

And I'm undone.

CHAPTER 14

SO ANXIOUS

THEM: 1999

You couldn't tell by the looks of the broad-shouldered and tree-tall nineteen-year-old Kyrie that he had only been with two girls. There was quiet Neece during his freshman year of high school. They grew up together and thought it made sense to try the sex thing together too. It didn't make sense. And it wasn't good. Then there was Sheree, the girl he had a crush on all junior year who threw up on him while they were having sex.

He didn't get to finish.

So he started to take his time with girls. And for some of them, it was too long.

But not for Amaya. She didn't realize he even liked her for months. She thought they made okay scene partners, but beyond that? She had her eyes set on getting to Hollywood, by hook, crook, or magic spell.

So it was as much a surprise to her when she looked up eight months after that fateful day in Professor Randall's class that she and Kyrie were together.

And she loved the shit out of him. He became her muse. Starring in her student projects, starring in the romance of her life.

And Kyrie never wanted to leave her side. She was the Nina Mosley to his Darius Lovehall.

So for their first time being together, he wanted it to be extra special. They were still living in dorms at Morgan, so he got a room at the Renaissance Hotel in downtown Baltimore. Fancy shit that cost him two overnight shifts at UPS. But he was happy to do it.

He went to Towson Town Center and got Amaya an engine-red lace teddy from Victoria's Secret. Picked it out himself with no sales associate assistance.

He got off work early, checked into the hotel, and began setting up. We're talking rose petals. Candles. A smallish boombox to play the slow jams CD he created and agonized over. But he was confident that starting with Ginuwine's "So Anxious" would set the right mood.

He was right. When Amaya arrived, she was overcome. No one had ever taken the time to build a romantic scene similar to those from her favorite movies. Kyrie had handled location, costume, production design, and music.

And he directed her to the bathroom. Undressed her. Then modeled for her while he sensually took off every piece of clothing he was wearing. He led her into the shower and with a freshly purchased loofah from Bath & Body Works, he washed her body like it was sacred and doing so was his blessing. Afterward, they kissed under the cascading water. She whispered in his ear, "Make love to me."

After drying her off, he led her to the bed, placing her ever so gently on the rose petals. She spread her legs for him. He entered so tentatively as not to hurt her because he's a solid nine inches. Allow me to repeat. Nine inches. Inch by inch, gently probing her entire circumference.

This was when Amaya learned that one of her spots is right at the entrance, missed by those so eager to plunge, without testing the waters. She wound her hips, he followed her rhythm. They danced together. She gripped his shoulders. His back. His ass. While he kissed her shoulders. Her neck. Her breasts. There were no fancy position switches, just the deepest of desires to feel one another, learn one another, enjoy one another, and finish one another.

And that's what they did. Twice that night.

CHAPTER 15:
CLICHÉ, CLICHÉ, CLICHÉ, CLICHÉ

AMAYA

I know. It's a rom-com cliche to slip out in the middle of the night. But I couldn't just spend the night at Kyrie's house. That would be silly. It was bad enough I had oral sex with an ex who abandoned me and popped up in my life decades later as a stand-in for my film. If I read that script, I'd judge the hell out of the female lead. Stupid, stupid girl.

But you would know none of this by the way I showed up on set today. A pep in my step. Prepared. Zena and I review my shot list for the day, mostly a montage of Lyric and Dante falling in love, which I completely redid last night because, well, I felt inspired.

"Okay, we're pushing it creatively today," Zena comments, game.

"I want to elevate our storytelling a notch."

Just then, he walks in for rehearsal, fresh haircut, a black tee that clearly didn't come in a pack, and perfectly fitting sweats. He looks better than he did last week. How is that possible?

"Good morning, director." And instantly I hear him call me that while between my legs.

"Good morning, Kyrie."

"How was your weekend?" He flashes a naughty smile.

"It was… uh… nice. Restful. Yeah." I look around at Zena and Yusef to see if they notice how I'm stumbling over my words like a cheating husband.

He waits for them to busy themselves with the plan for the day, then asks discreetly, "Are we good? You left without a word."

"Yeah. We're fine." I quickly excuse myself, telling him I had to get something back at video village.

"You're glowing!" Chloe says way too loud for my liking when I reach the monitors. It's also a cliché to be thought of as glowing after getting off. "You must have drank your water this morning," she surmises.

She doesn't know that I was baptized in Kyrie's waters. Born again.

"And you look cute." She means that I don't have on sweat pants and a vintage t-shirt, my set uniform. And no, I didn't put on a tank and jean shorts because of *him*. Okay, even I don't believe that.

"I took care of our problem."

"Which one?" I inquire because since we started filming, a bunch of them have popped up. Sub-par catering. Good food is a must for a happy crew. There was the P.A. who was posting movie spoilers on TikTok. And we still haven't found a location for our cafe.

She gets closer and leans in. "Found a new stand-in for Kyrie. Today will be his last day. I'll let him know after his last scene."

I hop up like I caught the Holy Ghost. "You can't fire him."

"What? You said you wanted him gone."

I let out a deep exhale, wait for a P.A. to pass by, then in the quietest whisper: "We messed around."

"Messed around how?"

"He went down on me," I say, half embarrassed and half turned on.

"Bitch what?" Chloe starts pacing and cracking her knuckles. Not a good sign. Means it's a big- ass problem that she doesn't yet know how to solve.

"You're jeopardizing what we worked years for? And you didn't even get any dick?"

Well, now she makes me sound extra silly. "That's not fair." Now we're both pacing.

"I can't fire him now. And how well do you even know him at this point? What if he's trying to exact some sort of revenge? Huh? He could sue, blackmail you, the sky's the limit for a come up."

"We are two consenting adults. And I wouldn't be the first director who got it on with an actor."

"YOU ARE A BLACK WOMAN. We are not the same as horny old white male directors who pat actresses on the ass and expect head from everyone."

I know that. And this is the biggest project of my life. Why am I risking it? Maybe part of me always wonders what would have happened if I didn't get on that plane. I love my career, don't get me wrong. But it's come with a lot of pain and heartache and sometimes I wonder what's the point of it all.

"What should we do?" I pose apprehensively.

Chloe stops pacing for a beat, but chews on her nails.

"Nothing. And by nothing, I mean, no more sticky icky with your ex. Do not smile, the briefest of hellos, matter of fact, just don't look in the brother's direction. We proceed, business as usual. Like nothing happened. And hope this goes away."

But what if I don't want it to go away?

CHAPTER 16

THIS IS SERIOUS

KYRIE

Finely chopped scallions. Tossed with fresh diced tomatoes. A dusting of rosemary. A dollop of salt. Cooking requires the same attention, care, and creativity as lovemaking. I put my back into it.

"Who's all this for?" Shani asks as she enters the kitchen without looking up from her phone, dressed like she goes to private school. She doesn't. I jump in her path so that she bumps into me.

"Dad!"

"I told you to watch where you're going."

"This is for us. How was school?"

Shani looks up, curious. She circles me. Inspects my haircut. Sniffs me like she's a German Shepherd at the airport. Lifts my hand to scrutinize my nails. Squints her eyes as she makes a final assessment.

"Who are you dating?"

I drain the Pappardelle and drizzle a little olive oil. "Dating? No. The director and I used to know each other. And it's been nice to see her again."

"You knew her before Mom?"

"Yeah. We went to college together."

Shani plops down on one of the island stools. Processes. Then she pops up.

"This is serious."

"Serious?"

"You have never talked about another woman besides Mom. Of course I know you smash chicks here and there."

"Shani!"

"But cooking and manicures? Yeah you like her. You like her a lot."

And in that moment, I settle into how much I like Amaya. *This* Amaya. Grown, successful, writer/director Amaya. Assured Amaya. Seasoned, delicious Amaya.

I sit beside Shani. Put my arm around her.

"How would that make you feel?"

"Like my dad will finally get a life."

I kiss her on the forehead, then serve our plates. She fills me in on the aftermath of getting into it with Brenda. Apparently they patched it up and are cool again. It's admirable. I wish it was that easy in adulthood. Amaya and I shared an exceptional night, but she ghosted before morning hit and I wouldn't say we're all patched up.

After we finish dinner, Shani heads to her grandmother's house for the weekend, and I call Amaya's hotel. The front desk patches me through and she answers on the third ring.

"Hello?"

"Hey. It's Kyrie."

"Kyrie?"

"I realized I didn't have your cell number. I looked for it on the crew list, but it wasn't listed. Are you hungry?"

"Why?"

"I made some of my world famous short rib ragu and can bring you some."

An excruciatingly long pause. The kind that makes you feel like a complete ass for thinking this was a good idea.

"Look, what went down, went down. But we need to keep things strictly professional here on out. Okay?"

"Yeah. Of course," I agree quickly to cover. We hang up. I sit for a beat, then I get up and head out.

I arrive at Amaya's hotel where all the producers are staying, leave the tupperware of pasta, a pack of fresh compression socks, and a note that reads, *"For my favorite director"* with the front desk.

She's not getting rid of me that easily.

CHAPTER 17

DAILIES

AMAYA

One am. That weird time of night. Not completely past the hump of the day, but far enough to release its angst.

With my glasses on, I watch, pause, rewind, the dailies from yesterday's shoot. It's a way for me to critique my own work. This scene between Lyric and Dante where they hang out with friends, and get into their first lover's quarrel, could have benefited from slower movement from the camera. To demonstrate the gentle unfolding of the perceived perfection of their relationship. It always happens subtly. Slight rips. Missed tears. I should have given a note to Ranita to play Lyric with even more ambivalence. An emotion that, if left untreated, slowly turns into resentment. Tomé's performance is pitch perfect, so much so that my heart twinges.

I nibble on the rest of the short rib ragu that he left for me. I want to be mad that he didn't listen to me. But all I am is smitten. He remembered my affinity for compression socks. The short rib is delicious. He's playing this really, really well.

I return to watching the dailies. I fast-forward and he steps into frame. I freeze it. Stand-ins aren't normally included in dailies. Divine intervention? Who knows, but I revel in it. I gaze upon him without pressure or looking over my shoulder. I explore every little detail of his frame. Rediscover every little detail of *him*.

Flashes of our night together bombard me. His lips grazing past my breast. I can taste the salt from his face after I licked it. I want him to consume me. Swallow me whole. Absolve me. Jesus. I slide my hand onto my honey pot. Heat radiates from her. I graze my finger across my clit, imaging that it is his thick tongue. I should have ordered that emergency vibrator.

Fuck this. I call *him*.

His bedroom. I don't venture too deep into it before he comes to me. He grabs my hands and places them on his body. He's so goddamn solid. And he doesn't drop my gaze. He also doesn't touch me. He lets me take the lead. So I do, by unbuttoning his shirt and taking it off. Then I unbuckle his pants, pull them and his boxers down to the floor. Lawd, I forgot how enormous and pretty his dick is. I covet that thang for a beat. He steps back so I can take him in. Perfection. He waits patiently for a nod from me. I offer it like a boss. Then he picks me up and carries me over to his custom platform bed. Places me down. Undresses me with the utmost care... I relax into it. He takes a beat to idolize my *entire* body. The non-child-bearing fupa. The wall of skin that hangs over my fibroid surgery scar. The fatty titties.

Then he puts on a condom like a pro. I pull him toward me and he enters me like he's home. And fucks me ravenously. He opens my legs wide and goes in and out, with great tease and restraint. Then he flips me over and I drop to my stomach so he can plunge the depths of me.

"Damn, Amaya."

"You feel that?" is all I can offer in the moment.

I've got him captivated and captured. Until, in one swift move, he turns me back over, picks me up and fucks me standing. This man is STRONG. He carries me over to the dresser and positions me on top of it. We pump together, a combination of heat, passion, and perfect angling catches me and I cum, loudly, wildly which turns him the fuck on. And turns me the fuck on. He pumps faster, hitting my spot, and as I'm cumming again, feeling his dick throbbing within me, he lets out an intense groan and cums with me. I've never had multiple orgasms. I always thought it was a myth that haters used to make you feel inferior. We collapse on each other. Sweaty. Satisfied. That shit was FUCKING GOOD.

GOOD FUCKING.

And now I'm really fucked.

CHAPTER 18

DO THE RIGHT THING

KYRIE

Antique shops. A general store. Old-timey post office. We're in a section of Ellicott City, a suburb of Baltimore, that feels like we're in a small town in a Nancy Meyers movie. Ironically, Amaya put me on to that director back in the day. I don't see shit about myself in her stuff, but the houses are always dope and casting is on point.

It took some goading and damn near blackmail, but I'm taking Amaya to a Bed & Breakfast owned by one of my former clients for lunch. I told her that she deserves a break and that research shows that rest and leisure helps with creativity. I don't have any stats to back that up, but figured it had to be true.

She gazes out of the window, a calm over her. I want to know what she's thinking. Fantasizing about our lusty last night? Then she turns toward me. *"Do the Right Thing* or *Malcolm X?"* she curiously poses.

I should have known she was thinking of movies. "Ah, see, you're playing dirty."

"It's a legitimate one."

"On one hand, *Do the Right Thing* is a perfect movie. Groundbreaking. On the other, *Malcolm X* is iconic. One of Denzel's best performances. Uggh… I'm gonna have to go with *Malcolm X*."

"Oh! It's *Do the Right Thing* all the way for me. You said it. Perfect movie. But also you really see Spike establishing his filmmaking aesthetic and voice."

"Okay, I have one for you. *Collateral* or *Heat*?"

"*Heat* all day."

After debating the craft of Michael Mann and his directing relationship with top talent, we arrive. Yvette, the owner, meets us at the door. I introduce Amaya as my director. Yvette fangirls over Amaya and they have one of those "we've never met but we love each other" Black women moments.

Yvette takes us on a tour of her beautiful mid-century modern home that she converted into a business. Yes, I managed the renovation. And yes, Yvette sings my praises as she walks us around. And yes, Amaya is impressed. But that's not the only reason I brought her here. We reach a back room, the hotel's restaurant.

"I overheard that you all lost a cafe location. Wondered if this would work?"

Amaya explores the space. Peering up at the high ceilings. Inspecting the plush furniture. Smoothing the wallpaper and the velvet drapes.

"It's perfect. I love it."

And I love that she loves it. "I'm just gonna need a location credit," I jokingly add.

"My place is about to star in a movie?!" Yvette's over the moon. "I just want to meet Ranita and Tomé and you can have it for free." She motions us over to one of the tables to sit down. "I'm going to grab some menus." Yvette heads to the back. Amaya and I settle into our seats.

"This is really sweet, for real. I didn't expect this."

"I just wanted to help."

"Well, you saved the day. I'm texting Chloe right now." Amaya shoots off a quick message.

"You should have seen the room before me and my team got our hands onto it. Oddly-placed columns, low ceiling, no windows."

"You all really transformed it. It's lovely."

"Thank you. It always reminded me of our first off campus date."

"At Cafe Raven. We shared a chocolate croissant."

"I was so broke."

"That didn't matter. We made it work."

"I guess we did."

"No, we did."

And all I can think about in the moment is, can we still?

• • ● • •

After Yvette's place, we strolled Main Street in Ellicott City. Got egg nog ice cream from the Creamery and sat on a bench watching the trolley come and go while making up stories about boarding passengers.

"He collects something weird, like dead bugs."

"Definitely," I concur with her assessment of a toupee-wearing bodybuilder type.

"What about her?" Amaya asks about a striking sister studying her phone.

"She's an artist. A painter. But before that, she was a burnt out lawyer."

"Defense attorney," Amaya adds. "Great money, but it ate at her conscience."

"Damn, you're really good at this." I compliment her storytelling skills. And I'm not just gassing her up. Her imagination is incredible. Sexy.

"I've had a lot of practice over the years," she replies modestly.

"You've done more than practice," I tell her. "You've mastered your craft."

"I'm no master. I still have a lot to learn."

"I get it. But don't sell yourself short. I know it may have taken time to get to your first feature, but you've been a visionary for decades."

She turns to me and no lie, she looks at me like I'm Eddie Murphy and she's Halle Berry in one of my favorite scenes from *Boomerang*. Halle's character had stayed late to help Eddie clean up after dinner. They're on the couch, watching television, falling asleep, and then bam. They start kissing.

Amaya kisses me, and shit, I melt. I didn't even know that was possible. But I do. Without shame. Her lips taste like strawberries. Sweet. Juicy. Nourishing. And yes, I close my eyes.

We seem to open our eyes together. She smiles at me like this is our normal.

And I hope it is.

But I can't rest on just one surprise. I have another trick up my sleeve.

About an hour or so later, we pull up to Morgan's campus.

"Really?" Amaya throws her head back, already amused.

"Had to take it back to where it all started." I hop out of the car, scurry to her side. Offer her my hand to escort her on a mini tour. The school is pretty empty, a few students and workers here and there.

"I can't believe how much Morgan has grown." Amaya surveys all the upgrades in awe. Modern glass buildings. New residence halls. Sprawling greens.

"They just got like 335 million dollars from the state, thanks to Governor Moore, to build a science and research center."

"Go 'head, Morgan. Big things. I was here maybe five years ago. Did a keynote for the Black Student Union. And to see that they keep growing makes me happy." She becomes contemplative for a moment.

"Sometimes I feel disconnected," she shares unexpectedly. "Like parts of life and the world are moving right along and I'm in this little bubble. And sometimes I'm not sure why."

I let her admission settle for a bit.

"I think that bubbles are meant to be burst, right?" I was hoping to come up with something a little bit more clever.

"You're trying to burst my bubble?"

"Do you want me to?" I lower my lips toward hers.

She pushes me away as we both laugh.

"Seriously, I get what you're saying. I feel like I created a box for myself. About what I could and couldn't do. What I should and shouldn't do. Especially as a man."

We both take in what I'm saying.

"Sometimes, only sometimes, I feel bad for y'all," she tells me. "Men. Society and gender norms don't leave much room for deviation."

"You're right. It's only been the last few years that I've allowed myself to push the corners of my box a little bit here, a little bit there. I've tried more things, took more risks, shit I even shed a tear watching the second *Black Panther*."

"Now you're taking it too far." She starts laughing.

I start overexplaining. "Chadwick. You know…"

"I'm just kidding," she reassures me. "For real, I'm glad you're expanding and feeling your feelings. And I bawled like a baby when I heard about Chadwick."

We share a moment of silence.

"You were never a crier."

"You're not the only one expanding." She flashes one of those undeniable smiles.

We approach Banneker Hall. She stops walking when she realizes where we are.

"I can't believe it's still here. It looks exactly the same."

"They haven't touched it. Basement is still stank as hell."

Amaya brightens.

"First one there wins." Amaya takes off before I can even really process what's going on. And she's faster than I imagined. I start running, but she had too much of a head start. She's panting and cracking up at the entrance when I make it there.

"I don't know why I did that," she admits, mid-giggle.

"I want a do-over." I mean this with every bone in my body. I want another chance with this woman. My declaration doesn't get past her. She nods kindly, but doesn't offer a response before heading inside.

We reach the basement and it's dark. Not horror-movie dark, but enough for Amaya to gently hold onto me. I guide her to Professor Randall's old classroom.

Where it all started.

Where we first met.

When we bonded over our love for movies.

Our meet cute.

When she first fluttered in my heart.

When I realized she's the smartest woman I've ever known.

When I showed her my passion for acting.

When she said I was good.

I flip on the lights and it's like we're transported back to 1998. Same raggedy desks. Worn chalkboard. It's perfect.

"This is a trip." Amaya takes out her phone and starts snapping pictures. "Let's shoot a movie," she says matter-of-factly before pointing the camera at me.

"You're already making a movie."

"*We're* making a movie. You're part of the crew too." Am I blushing at her including me in her dream?

Let's make another one," she adds. She begins moving the camera poetically, like a skilled Steadicam Operator.

"What's our movie about?"

"You tell me."

She's putting me on the spot. I smooth my chin, lick my lips. Then I drop into character.

I begin performing a monologue she wrote for me in like 2000 for the school talent show. It's about a young man who's in love with his best friend, but she doesn't know it.

"How much do I love thee? Let me count the ways. Nah, nah. Y'all would be here all day."

For a beat, Amaya lowers the camera. I can see it on her face. She can't believe I remember her words.

"Sometimes I just want to thank her Momma. That's how fine she is." I make the empty desks my audience. You can't tell me my ass ain't on Broadway somewhere. I play to the camera, but don't speak directly to it. It's a dance Amaya and I are doing. A lyrical one. Seductive even. She is behind me now, recording the back of me.

"But she's smart too. Like some kind of genius." I pause, look off for dramatic effect. I realize that I still have it. The passion. The talent. The ability to remember my lines. So I go for it.

"Genius doesn't even capture it all. What's bigger, badder, more creative than a genius?"

We go on like this for almost an hour.

And I love every minute of it.

"You light up the frame," she tells me not even a second after I finish.

"That means a lot coming from you."

"You always did. And you still do. I hope you continue getting back to your acting."

Now she really wants a brother to cry. But I keep it together.

"Thank you," is all I can muster.

"Thank you. For bringing me here. To my past."

"*Our* past," I correct her.

"Our past." She gives in. So I pull her to me. Close to me. And we start to sway to the sound of our own hearts beating.

We lie in my bed facing each other… just talking. About any and everything. Catching up over the last twenty years, before we get into the burning stuff.

"We never married. I think we were both scared of disappointing each other." I open up about Shani's mother, Erin. And surprisingly, it isn't weird. Feels like I'm talking to a friend.

"What about you? Any great loves?" I watch Amaya scan across her life, before ultimately ending at a no.

"I was with one guy, another director, for a couple of years."

"How was that?"

"I wouldn't do it again. He was always in competition with me."

"I already know he wasn't winning that."

"I kept getting work and he became more and more resentful."

"Damn."

"Yeah… but film has always been my great love."

We let that truth settle between us.

I brush her cheek with the back of my hand. She closes her eyes for a beat, then opens them with a smile.

"So does your mother still hate me?"

"Yes."

We both crack up over that one.

Then continue talking until the sun reminds us of the time.

· · ● · ·

We're making breakfast. Doesn't that sound so right? *We're* making breakfast. Late night sexing turned into a weekend-long date.

And she's wearing one of my t-shirts and a pair of my balling shorts. I feed her some of my summer fruit salad. She savors it.

"Do you have any Tajin?"

"Is that an LA thing?"

"Very much so. It's great on fruit." She leans in and kisses me. Like this is our daily morning routine.

And that's when Shani surprises the shit out of us. Amaya jumps slightly.

"Hey Dad!" Shani gets a kick out of it.

"Shani, honey, what are you doing back so early? You were supposed to come home from your grandmother's tomorrow evening."

Shani shrugs, with a big smile on her face. "Grandma wanted to go to Atlantic City and I didn't want to go. And her air conditioning isn't working. Who's this?"

"She dropped you off? I'll call her later, check in."

Shani nods, all smiley toward Amaya.

"Hi, I'm Amaya." Amaya waves. Embarrassment coloring her face.

"That's such a pretty name. Are you the director?"

Amaya glances at me. "Yes."

"Nice to meet you. I've heard so much about you."

"Really? Okay. Well, your father raves about you."

"What are we eating?" Shani plops into the chair. Back to life.

I can read Amaya's thoughts before she even utters them.

"I should probably get going." She smiles graciously before hauling out of the kitchen and upstairs.

Shani watches, then turns to me. "Well, damn. You gonna go after her?"

I probably should.

But I don't.

This is my life. And make believe is just that.

CHAPTER 19

SLO-MO

AMAYA

"I don't know what we're doing."

"I can tell you exactly what you're doing. Courting trouble."

Chloe and I are reviewing the reels of potential editors in my hotel room.

"I like his style, pretty seamless."

"Are we talking about your ex or the editor?"

"The editor! I'm just enjoying Kyrie's company. Although I did meet his daughter this morning, which I was not expecting to do, so I got out of there as fast as I could."

Chloe's eyes widen. "Meeting family?! And ignoring my guidance to stay the F away from him."

"He wouldn't do anything crazy like take legal action."

"You say that now, and then next thing you know, we're in court." She catches herself. She knows she's being harsh. "Look, he seems like a great guy. And like he wants you to win. Just be careful."

That's the thing. I feel like careful is all I've been when it comes to matters of the heart. All to avoid heartbreak. But it's no way to live and definitely no way to enjoy the living.

Chloe's phone buzzes. She answers and her face drops.

"Benji's downstairs. He needs to talk to us."

We rush to the lobby bar. I don't change. I'm sweat-panted and hoodied. Benji's there in a serious conversation with Yusef, waving his hands animatedly. This isn't good. I beeline to him. Chloe's on my New Balances.

"Tomé has Covid."

You know how everything goes slo-mo in movies? That's what's happening right now. Benji keeps talking, but his mouth drags. I don't understand him. But it immediately hits me what this means.

"Benji, we can shoot other scenes, rework the schedule. We don't have to shut down."

He looks at me quizzically.

"Yusef says there aren't any scenes to switch around. He says you had him shoot all of Ranita's scenes without Tomé early in the schedule." Benji wants a reason. A logical one. Not *I lost it seeing my ex and had to rearrange the schedule to avoid seeing him.*

"Um, yeah, I wanted to give Ranita and Tomé time to build authentic chemistry." I turn away, shame overcoming me.

"Well, I hope it was worth it. You're shut down. Five days. Studio protocol." Benji loves wielding this kind of power.

"Will we be given more time to make up the lost days?" Chloe pleads.

"I have to talk to my bosses. My rough estimate says we're going to lose at least a million. I don't think they're going to want to spend more money shooting those scenes."

"But we need those scenes or we don't have a movie." Now I'm pleading.

"I know," Benji spits out.

I'm boiling over. *He's* ruined my movie.

CHAPTER 20:
CLASSIC

KYRIE

Amaya texted me that she wanted to see me. I wasn't sure how she felt about meeting Shani, since she bolted, so I was relieved to hear from her. I don't even get a chance to knock on her hotel room door when it flings open. She looks like she's been crying.

"You okay?"

She moves aside to let me in.

"You fucked up my movie," she alleges with disappointment and disgust. I'm hella confused. But she seems very clear and on edge.

"What's going on?" I inquire collectedly to try to calm her down.

"The studio shut us down. And you know why?" She gets in my face, pointing more than fingers. "Because you popped up out of nowhere after twenty years and I wasn't prepared for that, so I had to make adjustments. And now those adjustments have come back to bite me in the ass.

And I may not be able to shoot the scenes we'll lose over the five days we're shut down. My movie is going to be an incoherent mess *if* it's ever released. So yeah, you ruined my movie! It's ironic, you know, that now you want to show up. Because you sure as hell didn't when it mattered." She turns her back on me. An action that's as triggering as her words.

I hit back. "I asked you for more time. To get my shit together before moving across the country to expensive-ass LA and you said nah. After four years of showing you my heart, you decided I wasn't worth waiting for. You left me!" I hold back the *Glory* tear that wants to roll down my face.

"Classic, blame everything and everyone else for your cowardice. Admit it. You were too scared to bet on us and to bet on yourself. And now decades later you've grown some courage. Well, too late."

That one hurt. But I don't back down. "What do you want from me, huh? You act like I've been in this by myself."

"I can't believe I thought this time would be different."

I regain my senses. I don't want to fight with her. I get close to her.

"Look, I'm so sorry this is happening. Maybe I can help?"

"Yeah, by staying the fuck out of my life."

And as fast as she was back in my life, she's gone again.

CHAPTER 21:

SLOW DOWN, MORE TIME

THEM: 2003

Their first adult apartment was the size of a big closet, but Amaya and Kyrie never complained. It was safe, cheap, and clean, save for the roach incident that almost took both of them out. They made it a home. Amaya bought some plants from Giant's, the local grocery store, that she managed to keep alive for the entire year they lived together. Kyrie did all the cooking, whipping up a variety of Rachel Ray dishes that would last them the week.

But now the apartment was boxed up. They were moving out.

Amaya was a ball of energy. Nonstop moving and talking. "I hope I can find a good hair dresser in LA. I'm not trying to look a mess out there."

Kyrie on the other hand, was unusually quiet as he over-taped a box.

"Good that you learned how to cut your own hair so you don't have to find a barber." Amaya was considering everything.

"Amaya." Kyrie stopped his excessive taping.

"Oh, I forgot to tell you. An actress I met in an AOL Chat room recommended a couple of temp agencies for me to check out."

"Amaya."

"Yes?"

"Slow down."

"Sorry. You know how I get when I'm excited." She patted a few boxes for no reason.

"I mean. Can we slow down? I need more time."

"To pack?"

"No, more time… here."

It started to click for Amaya.

"We talked about this, Kyrie, and we agreed that we were ready to move."

"I know. But I thought about it more, and–"

"You thought about it more? Our flight leaves tomorrow."

"We can change the tickets."

Amaya slinks onto a box. "For when? How much time are we talking?"

Kyrie shrugs. He doesn't want to say.

"How much time, Kyrie?"

"A year or two?"

Amaya couldn't fucking believe what she was hearing. She popped up. Rubbed her temples. Smoothed her bob. Slowly dragged her hands over her face.

"We put a deposit down on an apartment."

"Maybe we can get it back." Kyrie kept shifting uncomfortably on the box he was sitting on.

"Where is all this coming from?" Amaya was trying really hard to understand.

"I wanna stack more dough."

"Kyrie, we have savings and we're gonna get jobs."

"What if we can't?"

Amaya leans her head on a box. "I don't know what to tell you, Kyrie. I'm not staying here another year. We have a plan and I'm ready. I'm gonna get some air." Amaya walked out, not realizing that it was the beginning of the end.

Amaya gnawed on her nails while her shaking leg kept bumping her suitcase. She peered at the empty seat next to her. In fact, it was empty all around her, save for the airline attendant who watched over her with pity, until she couldn't any longer.

"Ma'am, we need to close the doors now."

Amaya nodded while tears started rolling down her face. She gave hope a few more seconds. Then she gathered her things and got on the flight to Los Angeles.

Without *him*.

CHAPTER 22

WAITING TO EXHALE

AMAYA

Several packs of Chips Ahoy cookies, a wine bucket with two bottles in it, and our resolve are sprawled on my bed. Chloe and I are laid out looking like we've been cast in *Waiting to Exhale*.

"Well, look at it this way, no one can hate a movie that never sees the light of day." Chloe offers a bright side. I will take any ray of sunshine I can get right now.

"And they won't be able to say that I shit my first feature film."

"Exactly!" We toast our round hotel glasses that are filled to the rim.

"I'm proud of you," Chloe adds.

"Now you're taking it too far."

"You chose yourself over work for once."

I put my glass down on that one.

"Chloe, I slept with our stand-in. And you were pissed about it."

"I was, but he also happens to be the love of your life. For twenty years, you and I have sacrificed everything to make it in Hollywood. We've had some wins, but this business is unrelenting, toxic as fuck, and damn sure doesn't love us back. But I saw how that man looked at you, with pure adoration."

"That's a big word."

"And it honestly doesn't capture the fire between y'all. We've had to do and say all the right things, even when it went against our better judgement in order to be seen by these execs. Sometimes having someone else see us helps us see ourselves."

Well damn. I guess she told me.

"Since it doesn't look like we have a movie, can I bag that twentysomething thick slim boom operator now?" Chloe shimmies.

I can only laugh. Somehow, I know that everything is gonna be okay.

•• • ••

And everything was okay. Over our third bottle of wine, Chloe and I devised a brilliant idea to hit up every person with money we came to know over our time in Hollywood: actors and actresses, politicians, athletes, business owners, relatives, enemies, and asked each for a $10K pledge. We had more than $600,000 in pledges. We shared the list with Benji who shared it with his higher-ups. The heavyweight support encouraged the studio to give us the money we needed to finish our film.

So I'm back in my director's chair. And it feels damn good. But incomplete. I look around for *him*. Hoping tensions have thawed and maybe we can… I don't really know. I just know I'm finally ready to put our past behind us.

But in that moment, another stand-in steps into frame.

And I've lost *him* once again.

CHAPTER 23

NOT FOR SET

KYRIE

I'm headed out the door to meet up with Oscar. Back to work. Like nothing happened. Like I wasn't just taking part in my lifelong dream or like I wasn't just holding *her* in my arms.

"You're wearing that?" Shani asks as I come downstairs. She's backpacked and ready for school.

"This is my normal uniform," I remind her.

"Not for set."

I pause, unsure the best way to break the news to her. "I'm no longer working on the film."

"Why?"

"It wasn't for me."

"What about Ms. Amaya?"

"We're not working together anymore."

"Are you fucking kidding?"

"Language, Shani."

"No. You always do this. Self-sabotage." She gets in my face.

"What?

"You been wanting to act for like forever. And you finally stop being a scaredy cat and do it and now you're no longer working on the film? And then, you finally find a woman who you care about without feeling guilty about Mom, and you mess that up?!"

Well damn. I guess she told me. I put my bag down and slink down to the arm of the couch. She's right and the truth hits me like the bricks I use in renovations.

She sits beside me, puts her hand on my shoulder like any responsible parent. "I love you and all, but it's time to get your head out of your ass."

And with that much needed pep talk, I do just that.

CHAPTER 24

ONE TAKE

AMAYA

The director's role is to bring out the best performances in everyone, not just cast. At least that's how I see it. It's a shame I can't do it in real life.

I haven't called *him*. Instead, I've just been watching the "movie" I shot of him on Morgan's campus like it's reruns of *Living Single*.

It's the last day of shooting and the remainder of the shoot has gone disturbingly smoothly. Zena and I got some amazing shots. Ranita and Tomé crafted dazzling performances. The studio has seemingly moved on from our shutdown, so much so that Benji flew back to LA. But that feeling of incompleteness that creeped in has now burrowed itself deep within me. So I've been filling it with what I know best, busyness, above and beyond, finishing the shoot. I've been reading scripts for our next project, reworking my shot list five and six times, overwatching dailies. And counting down the days until I'm back in LA.

Which is apropos because we're shooting the last scene of the movie today. How beautifully poetic. Or beautifully tragic.

"We made it!" Chloe shimmies beside me.

"Yeah, but if we don't nail this scene–"

"Can't you celebrate for one moment?"

Sure can't. Have you ever watched a movie, and kind of enjoyed it, but the last scene fell so short that it ruined the entire movie? Or have you watched a movie that was just okay, but the last scene was so perfect that it made you love the movie?

This is where we are. So Ranita and I have been working a lot on the scene, to dig into the emotion of it all, since it is just her, at the airport, waiting.

I ask that the set be pin-drop quiet. I want Ranita to be so immersed in the pain of the moment when she realizes that Dante is not showing up.

We're close on her face. It fills the frame. Her eyes are heavy with yearning. It's heartbreaking. And for a beat, I'm transported back to that airport. Everyone's waiting on me to call action. Chloe nudges me, but I close my eyes, and absolve myself of the guilt, the what-ifs, and the regrets. I mouth to young Amaya, *It's going to be okay. You can get on the flight.* I open my eyes. I'm ready now.

"Action." The camera slowly pushes in on our Lyric, her eyes watering, her teeth clenching her bottom lip. The beats that pass are excruciating. And just as she's about to get up, Dante comes running in.

I may have done a minor rewrite.

And I didn't tell anyone, including Ranita. Her response—the sparkle in her eyes, the widened mouth—is completely real. The awestruck. She runs into his arms. He swings her around. Then the flight attendant suggests they finish their reunion on the plane so they can take off.

It's a perfect scene. A happy ending.

I only need one take.

"Cut!"

The set explodes. Chloe and I fall into each other's arms amidst high-fives and whoos!!

"You sneaky dog! You changed the ending!" Chloe beams with pride.

"We did it," I finally say. And another tight, emotional hug between us.

As I spin around, there he is. He has been watching the entire time. I don't know what came over me, but I run to Kyrie like I'm starring in a rom-com. His arms engulf me.

"I'm sorry," spills out of our mouths at the same exact time.

"I want to try again," he declares with so much conviction.

"I would like that." He kisses me like a prince to applause and a chorus of "awwws."

I couldn't have directed a better scene for us.

I might just get my happy ending after all.

ABOUT THE AUTHOR

Felicia Pride is a TV writer/producer and an award-winning filmmaker. She's written on QUEEN SUGAR, GREY'S ANATOMY, and BEL-AIR and has developed television shows for the likes of Amazon, Netflix, and FX.

In film, Felicia's the writer and executive producer of REALLY LOVE, which debuted on Netflix and became a Top Ten Movie on the platform. Her romantic drama features DEEPER and LIKE IT'S THE LAST are both in development at Universal. Felicia made her directorial debut with tender, an award-winning short film which aired on STARZ, and helmed LOOK BACK AT IT, a proof of concept for her directorial feature debut by the same name, which won the audience award at the BlackStar Film Festival and was nominated for an Humanitas Prize for screenwriting.

Felicia founded and runs HONEY CHILE, an independent media + production company catering to Black women 40+ and is the host of their podcast IT'S GOOD OVER HERE, a followup to their twice NAACP Image Award-nominated podcast Chile, Please.

Felicia's career in media and entertainment has spanned almost twenty-five years. Prior to writing for the screen, her career included roles in marketing, distribution, impact, editorial, and education. Felicia is considered a "Swiss army knife" because of her unique, multifaceted experience as a storyteller, marketer, and entrepreneur.

Felicia has helped thousands of writers and other storytellers thrive creatively, especially those who are marginalized, through her former platform The Create Daily. These days, she continues to support historically excluded storytellers through HONEY CHILE's educational arm, The Sweet Build.